"She's a big girl now," her daddy thought,
"and I guess that is okay."

"But she's still my little princess,
and that will never go away."

So up he ran to tuck her in,
all snuggled in her bed.

He leaned in close to hug her tight
and gently kissed her head.

But then he heard from the top of the stairs
a voice call down to him:

"Come on, Daddy! Hurry up!
Aren't you going to tuck me in?!"

He thought of all that she would do,
everywhere that she would go.

Of all the things that lay ahead,
everyone whom she would know.

And so her daddy watched her go,
just like his princess asked.

And with each stair his princess climbed,
his mind was racing fast.

"I'm not scared. I won't fall.
I don't need any help."

"Daddy, I'm a big girl.
I can do this by myself."

"Daddy, I'm a big girl.
You don't have to carry me."

"Put me down. I can do it.
Just watch and you will see."

That's when the princess spoke the words
he didn't want to hear.

An unexpected sentence
that filled Daddy's heart with fear.

The princess had grown tired,
and said, "It's time for bed."

He swooped right in and picked her up
and threw her overhead.

And then one night it happened...

No matter what, this always was
his favorite time of day.

When he held her softly in his arms,
the world would melt away.

With big, strong arms he would pick her up
and whisk her off to bed.

Then gently lay her down to sleep,
and sweetly kiss her head.

And soon this little princess
would do so much on her own.

Except the one thing Daddy did
since the day he brought her home.

She loved to play, spin in her dress,
and laugh, and dance, and sing.

This little princess loved all the world
and every living thing.

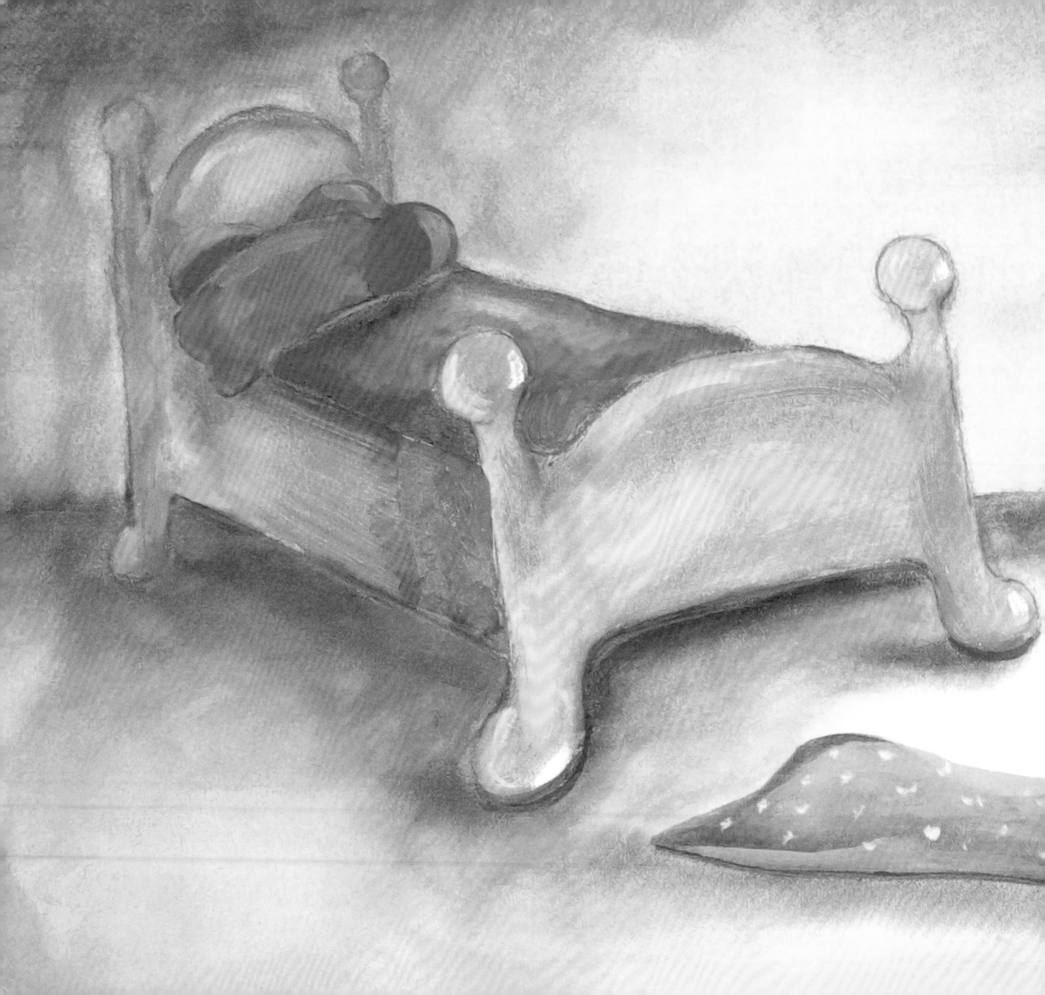

He watched her grow, learn to crawl,
then stand up tall to walk.

And in no time this little girl
would talk, talk, talk, talk, talk...

A little girl came into the world
and captured her daddy's heart.

She held it there in her gentle hands
right from the very start.

I'm a
Big
Girl

A Story for Dads and Daughters

Written by Greg Pope
Illustrated by Lea Wells